RAIN FROM

RAIN FROM A CLEAR BLUE SKY

Poems
by
~~Mercer Simpson~~

Mercer Simpson

To Marian
Best wishes for Christmas 1994
Mercer

GOMER

First impression—1994

ISBN 1 85902 192 1

© Mercer Simpson

This volume is published with the support of the Welsh Arts Council.

Printed by J.D. Lewis & Sons,
Gomer Press, Llandysul, Dyfed

For Betty and Jane with love
and in memory of Ian

ACKNOWLEDGEMENTS

Two-thirds of these poems originally appeared in the *Anglo-Welsh Review*, the *New Welsh Review, Poetry Wales, New Prospects Poetry, Social Care Education, BWA* and *Nonsuch*. In addition, 'In Barbara Hepworth's Sculpture Garden, Trewin, St. Ives' was reprinted in *Hepworth: A Celebration, ed.* David Woolley (Westwords, 1982).

Also by Mercer Simpson
East Anglian Wordscapes (poetry)
(with drawings by Miriam King)
The Rockingham Press, April 1993

Contents

Contents (*continued*)

CHILDHOOD'S
COUNTRY

A Sheltered Upbringing

The whole earth is our hospital
Endowed by the ruined millionaire
(*T.S. Eliot: East Coker*)

I.

First I thought
that at the porter's lodge
with the hospital gates
closed, the world ended.
Inside, the groomed lawns
were not for playing on,
the circular flowerbeds
were not for laughter:
what grew up here
were never children.
Under the arches
of the main buildings'
red and yellow brick,
my furtive hide-and-seek.
Above, windows were barred
but not to screams
that puzzled sleep
and fractured the night
of doves and owls
in trees that screened the wards.
What went in, came out
of the house next door,
I never knew, too young
to read the notice on its wall:
Mortuary. At night
I read the stars above our house
and never counted up to death.

3

II.

With brick red faces glinting in the sun
forts punctuate the ridge above the hospital,
hunched shoulders on the skyline hidden under grass.
Their narrow eyes are slits for firing on fixed lines.
The gatehouse mouth is open wide:
drill sergeants' frenzy of command,
the clash of rifles in arms drill,
the clump of marching feet
on echoing tarmac, grated on by heels.
A limp flag flutters on a pole.
The sentry grumbles in his box.
The faces of the forts perspire.
They are toy forts, the soldiers lead
that will melt down or have their heads
snapped off, played with by time
and shrunken into distances
a child won't see so far below.
Bugles haul down the sun at last
that dips below the ridge
where lights will twinkle up among the stars.
The irony of forts
that look down on a hospital
and on my father's shellshock cases in the wards:
a child's hand cut by metal toys;
war wounded bleeding to slow death
from memories.

III.

Once the crest of the ridge
         was gained
my childhood world
         ended
would not follow
         the names on signposts
pointing north
         the view of cloudgrey
patchwork of fields
         exploring disappointment

The promised land was south
         across the water
to the island
         and over its hills
to imagined cliffs
         to where the sea
was endless
         for ships and birds
whose land dropped
         out of sight

IV.

Strange how the heart's
         tied to places
its pulse of warmth
         the blood's surge
beating like oars or wings
         through seas or skies
defined by a journey
         narrowing to the point

of return. The circulation
        revives fingers and toes
for me to write or run
        as I invent my own
nightmare sun.

V.

This garden's Einstein's universe.
Carroll foresaw it in his *Looking Glass*.
All paths bend back upon themselves,
return us neatly to our starting point,
simplistic paradigms of life.
The hope of journeys is a sun
beckoning from beyond the wall
in which there is no gate
but sky with scattered streaky clouds,
a line of trees in shuddering green
that whisper messages we cannot hear
too far downwind. Even bright day
has caged us in as once again
the house approaches, and the path
leads us up to the French
windows open wide. Inside
reflections in the fireplace mirrors
multiply into infinity.
Yet still we turn and walk away.
There is no time to stay indoors.

VI.

Like birthdays for the elderly
returns aren't always happy.
Not surprising how
the view's changed utterly.
Our house divided. Two front doors
rub shoulders underneath
a common lintel where a generous one
had space to open years ago.
The trees are nearly all cut down.
The garden's shrunken, jaded strips of lawn
faded to browned-off coarseness.
The summer house has gone
and in its place tall railings cage
an electricity transformer,
dangerous beast to stalk a childhood garden
through which a road runs where I played
so that the mortuary's on the other side.
I'd pitch my wigwam underneath the bars
on its secretive windows. No access now
to cross to death where ambulances shudder through
the ghosts of children and their toys,
the memories long dismembered
and stretchered off to Casualty.
Inside the house I dare not enter
knowing my footprint on the stairs
covers my own and my father's in the dust
and curtains tremble at no touch of hand;
my mother's voice is just too faint to hear.
All's letters that I couldn't join
and sentences I couldn't understand
aged five, in pencil, in my copybook.
Inside their walls the figures move away

into a half-forgotten scenery
until the present snaps its fingers,
a door closes quietly and the house
returns to two. I stand outside
a stranger to this place and time
I'll not be wandering in and out again.

Tramway up to Horndean

The tramway ground up the face
of scar-tissued hospital walls
and shuddered past the pale
grey faces of windows, the iron car's
raised arm clinging to the wire.
Breathing hard up the hill
and wide-hipped as a washerwoman,
the tramcar busybodied about,
clattering with gossip: its flanged
wheels whined against rusty rails
to judder to a stop
at our low wooden platform.
Partitioned off in his cab, the driver
sat hunched over his tram-handle,
faceless under his peaked cap,
a leaden toy cast in the same
mould as his machine.
I can't remember ever
going far in it,
the end of the line being a forbidden
territory of tramps and gipsies,
the destination board's magic word
I learned to read, *Horndean.*
Surely it climbed out of our world

into my Eden at the valley's end
attainable through arches of branches,
past villages whose secrets
underpinned the foundations of churches
or slept under thatch, where cottages'
reluctant faces peered through the glint
of flints, half-open window eyes
through whose inquisitive stare you'd ride
proud on the tramcar's upper deck,
at the terminus too suddenly bumped out
of childhood, down to the ground's
sea-shaken legs. Off on your own at last
in woods kneedeep in bluebells,
or stretching up for berries in hedgerows,
you'd be surprised how easily
gates to green fields swung open,
the path to beechen hangers cresting
the round downs with a picnic view for miles
windscorched and sunburnt on the summit.
At home, inside the window-bars and safe red brick
I never learned the names of flowers,
how to climb trees, collect birds'-eggs,
kept innocent of the smell of earth.
Instead, my copybook politeness
handed round tea and cakes whenever Matron called.
From my bedroom window, through the trees,
a glint of metal and a bell:
the years I lost go rattling past
and up the hill.

Manoeuvres on Portsdown Hill

O what are they doing with all that gear;
  What are they doing this morning, this morning?
Only the usual manoeuvres, dear,
  Or perhaps a warning.
                    (*W.H. Auden*)

The four beasts squatting on the ridge
have wrapped the skyline round their shoulders
and kept their heads down in the grass
through which their brick-red faces peer
squint-eyed to fire along fixed lines.
Each gaping gatehouse mouth
shouts orders from a dark interior:
drums, bugles and the flicker of a flag
like eyelid on wall eye; the glint of sun
on bayonets its teeth, a secret brightness.
At night, astride the ridge, the creatures ride
and raid through children's unsuspecting dreams
a shadowed territory to their north.
Returned to daylight's waking calm
at sunrise telescopes are trained
to sweep the ridge: the enemy
is never named.

                    A boy and girl
make circuitous approaches, spying out
the demarcation lines of love and war,
treading a minefield of their making.
Their roadside cycles lie in chained embrace.
Two hundred yards along the ridge,
scant cover on the hill's chalk scalp,
they keep their distance, hoping it's dead ground
they're lying in, grass whitened, thin

10

and beaten down by wind, and turning from the sun
(its burning-glass on body sweat)
see chalk-white contours in each other's face.

Commands are issued from the nearest fort,
patrols detailed to bring them in.
Interrogation cells lie further underground
each day scrubbed clean, devoid of furnishing.
The questioning's simplistic and routine:
names and addresses, no trespasses forgiven;
the padre's in attendance for confession.
No one's identified their sin.

The quarry's gone to ground, foxed, hunted out
of wind-scorched grass no one dare hide behind.
The landscape's tinder-dry. One careless move,
a spark will fire it, or a touch
knock out the pin of a grenade.
Recruits instructed on the rifle range
may be promoted to the firing squad.
Huddled together in a hollow out of sight
the two discover that they're making love.

Next day upon the ridge defaulters gather
spent cartridges that might be blanks;
a small white handkerchief's blood-stained;
fluttering on the grass a wounded bird
becomes a torn-out diary page
dated late August, 1939, entry
in Gothic script; not far away
the footprints aren't quite man or beast
though tyre-marks show where two have ridden off together.

II
CLASSICAL
STUDIES

A Warning from Icarus

Daedalus my father, brilliant engineer,
had it all plotted; escaping from the tyrant king,
the course we were to follow, elevation, height,
and where the thermals might give one uplift;
and then our wings' construction: feathers and wax,
like giant birds sweeping the blue void
hazing the hazardous winedark Aegean, leaving far behind
that labyrinth of guilt my father had designed.
Never would there be, I was assured,
an escape like ours, in myth or history.

But then I fell in love.
The lover struts, would be as Greek tragic actors are,
taller than stilts, louder than megaphone,
posing as hero or god for his secret audience of one,
the easiest pickings for that vulture death
that hovers over every lover, gambling on all
for the promise of a kindly word or smile.

This I determined, altering my father's plan:
Father, I said, to fly behind the Sun
surely is easy; time must be different there,
moving backwards through another dimension;
there will my giant wings
beat the unexplored air for time to stand still;
I shall become immortal as the gods.
And girls must love the gods. They have no choice.
Remember Leda, however strange a form
lustful Jove took, she couldn't help herself.
I'll go one better than he did, not mere swan
but aviator flying out of the sun
with all the heart's guns blazing
to shoot down all my rivals, even charioteer Apollo.

My father laughed, and gave me sane advice,
that there's a geometry in the heart
and even intuition finds its proofs
as water its own level.

I would not listen. Father, the girl I love, I said,
is as the Sun to me; my heart
must soar towards her in inevitable flight;
with such strange magnetism I can compass nothing else.
Such warmth there is in closeness to her
I dare not look at her: some have gone blind
staring too long into the Sun's relentless eye
transfixed by beauty to a self-destruction,
powerless to resist it, knowing all the time
that this would be and yet it had to be.
This is the mental posture of a lover.
Blinded because we see precisely what we want to see,
misapprehensions drive us to destruction.

So off I soared in flight alone,
shouting a last farewell
to the father too old to be a lover,
or too wise. How blind his eyes
yet keeping them averted from the Sun
he seemed to me to keep his measured course
until in sadness I had turned away from him.

My fate's so often been reported thus:
Flying-Officer Icarus,
missing, believed killed over the Aegean Sea,
perhaps shot down by an enemy
who came at him laughing out of the sun;
his possibly foolhardy gallant mission
certainly not completed;

disobedience of orders from his superior officer
may well have been the cause of failure;
if so, perhaps he might have faced court-martial,
only the dead can face no second firing-squad.

Now you have heard the version of officialdom,
allow me to tell my story for myself:
I flew on blindly in my heart's direction;
not even my lips to hers,
not even her soft hands' touch,
not even a short fond whisper of farewell
as my waxed wings melted to a fall
drowning me in a depthless sea
of silence.

From Hades, Father, forgive me my ambition.
Better to be an engineer than a lover,
even though I'm threatened with a turn on Ixion's wheel.
Challenging Apollo is the epitome of folly, though no sin
save that I threw away the life you made for me
the life for which you held such hopes for me.
The gods, when handsome, always win.

Postscript from Theseus

It took me ten years
to get to the heart
of the labyrinth
and then there was no
monster at home, only
a suspicious pile
of bones: difficult,
of course, to say to whom
these belonged—perhaps
the monster had died
out of boredom and loneliness,
starved of human contact.
Better this than to kill
an old monster, crippled
with age and useless memories.

No doubt it's like this
with love: look at all
that nonsense I wrote
about Icarus; what sort of
witness I was, unreliable,
prejudiced, with a fight
I shrank from on my mind.
And Ariadne became a bore.
I left for Athens.
The Aegean was a void
drained of its wine-dark,
the sea reflected drowning
monsters and beating wings
and had been bled white
into a flat calm.

Labyrinth

I

The building's purpose is mystery to the child.
Its eyebrow lintel frowns over a dark portal,
an open mouth from which he thinks he hears
as if from a whorled shell, waves of the sea,
rattle of pebbles shaken in the tides' bag,
or fog-moan of a distant sea-beast on a faint wind.
From the open door issues an uncoiling rope,
the umbilical cord inviting return to the womb,
the quest to find the place of beginning,
hauled up on a rope, bringing the ship into the wind.
Otherwise this passage will lead to the tomb
of a giant golden king alone in the darkness
enthroned in the midst of his useless treasures.
Another turn, the child runs southwards to the sun,
to August beaches, steamer at the pier,
blaze into opening light dazzling on cliff-face,
sparkling on quiet waves, freed from sea-cave.
Tunnels are telescopes of time and distance,
but there's no straight route through the labyrinth.
He must explore side-alleys, gamble time's pennies:
ghost train at a fair; tunnel of love;
always the wrong turn taken. Growing up
is to get lost in it.

II

The Labyrinth grows like body cells.
People inhabit it, scurry antwise
along its passages without apparent purpose

except to avoid each other, silent,
alienated as Londoners in the tube
at rush hour, each with his Walkman tuned in
to private business. One here carries
a cancer cell of multiplying ignorance,
another an unexploded device in his briefcase.
The Minotaur's disguised in pinstripe suit,
bowler hat, furled umbrella: convincingly faceless.
We can encounter him only alone. The others
will have left the carriage before the train
has reached its terminus. Then we shall know
it is for us that the dice have rolled awry, for whom
the odds-on favourite has fallen at the first fence,
whose ship struck the iceberg too far south
on her maiden voyage, for whom the irrational
tumour flared: for us the rope is sheared
off short, and the unarmed heart stops
as we face him alone in the dark
with no way out. Our epitaph
burdened with false heroics, should read
Unlucky, and reason waste no sense
on where no reason is.

Eumenides

Behind the curtains in the palace drawing room
concealed in swirls of drapery they assume
the body's contours; even when
shaken out to air they'll plot
the king my father's death,
their infinite presence glimpsed as three
faces in a gilt mirror before the glass shivered
leaving me with a small
wound that will never heal:
always just out of reach, the suppressed image
recurs, always stands behind me until
I look round stealthily
trying to catch them off guard,
but they've gone.
                  But the course of events
moves one degree off true, for the fatal error
infiltrates the computer, electronics
short-circuit, the airliner plunges to earth
in an incandescent spiral. Safe arrival
is never assured, one is looking over one's shoulder
into shuddering distances, listening for voices
carried away on the wind. If one could see their faces,
they would be those of friends, laughing.

An Appointment with Mithras

(Car accident, near Hadrian's Wall, midwinter)

Shaken like dice inside the somersaulting car
we three spilled out, uninjured treble six.
After black ice on a right-angle bend
we couldn't turn, had gone straight on,
smashed head-on through a hedge
as the road accelerated into the sky's
accusations of starlight. We missed
an upright railway sleeper by a foot
that would have sliced us all in half.
Earlier in the watery sunlight of the afternoon
we'd danced around the phallic symbol by the well
you'd excavated on the Wall
close to the Mithraic cistern where
the legion's converts lay
with honey on their chests
in freezing water. After this mockery
what price protection, let alone survival?
Mithras, you said, what have the gods in store?
I can't forget your terrible death
thirty years on. I still look back
on this day, this evening, wondering.
We huddled in the blindness of the dark,
uncertain where we were, dead or alive,
the car's headlights gouged out.
The rockhard ground had frozen to death.
This was no site for burial.
An apologetic moon rose, gaping over fields,
open-mouthed, uncomprehending, foolish.
We moved slow heads to recognise each other.

Homo Erectus, Cerne Abbas

Think of your age, old man:
keeping anything up too long
can lead to problems:
exhaustion, frustration,
brandishing that phallic club,
waiting for something exciting
or for someone that, like Godot,
never comes; that woman, now,
alleged to have been on your left hand,
who stood you up a thousand years ago,
she's invisible because she's been
put out to grass, even though
she must have got you going
at the beginning,
idol with feet of chalk
instead of clay, standing
two thousand years, the longest
erection in history.
On the smooth green curve
of downland above your head
the villagers would celebrate
the rites of May, young men
and virgins garlanded
in a deflorescent
expectancy; but little
satisfaction you must have got
out of it, but that they kept
your white lines sharp and clean,
nearly all flesh being grass
but memory evergreen.

Collected Poems

A semi-colon
near the end
of a long verse
paragraph;
confessing that
a life's work
approaches conclusion;
turning round
to lose Eurydice,
only the last flickers now
before the Bacchanalian
dismemberment. Why has he
come to prose
unsteady on metrical
feet, and not quite
sober? The imagery
so thin, the knife of wind
is through the ribcage.
His heart's already
buried elsewhere.

III
PEALS
AND
CHANGES

Peals and Changes

I

After Trafalgar, After Sedgemoor . . .

Laughers in ropes,
irregular convulsions
from steepleframed people.

Is it a victory
this music revisits
or the intricate
jingling of bone?

II

Dirge for a Marriage

The romping crosswires
do not convince
at the marriage of
the bellmouthed prince
with beggarmaid:

even the laughing
ringers are afraid:
the rhythm strung
on the arm trembles:
one nodding bell,

lust's frantic fumbles:
no sleep for a fool
nor a frightened girl.

III

Sermon Without Text

The warped spire
creaks in the rain;
the tower cracks
fingered by the wind;
the sanded foundations
pour into the hourglass:
the preacher's time
is upended.

For the resurrection
of dying faith
time unwinds its reversal
through the universal
black hole of unbelief.

IV

Seithennin at Cantre'r Gwaelod

Unlucky sentry dozing at dykewatch
when the loneliness that's history
turned its back for the tidal wave's breaking:
so his bones danced down the sunshafted fathoms
scoured out by the tide-race's flared spume of dragonheads;
the crunch of waves on the beach a clashing of battleaxes,
a trampling of shingle in the hissing dark,
charging to spring floods high over headlands,
engulfing all earthworks; Gwyddno's land crumbled
in a giant's fist with the treachery of light-fingered soil.

28

Sarn Gynfelin, causeway of a betrayed nation,
marches its line of prisoners into the sea,
each stone heart torn out and hurled at the dying sun
out of which the invisible enemy rowed
in blood that set in the west.

Legends ripple and multiply, sigh under seaswell,
the saltmarsh under the surges, the wavefingered bell
of the drowned church their beating pulse,
wreckmarkerbuoy of a nation's burial ground.

Who now for the confidence of the rebuilt tower,
to recast bells, redeem unbattlemented peals,
and find a heaven clear enough to hang them in
to consecrate one nation to its unborn peace,
piloting the undrowned lovers into haven?

V

Transmutations

Cracked bells are chalice-flowers
whose rusted iron melts down
into daffodil-gold
of honeyed tone
and history's strident clapper
wears to a silence too
unless its hanging man
no longer pulls at his bell-rope
catch-as-catch-can.
Under unceremonious burial

of collapsing stone
into weed-throttled pool
bell and clapper now become
fertilised flower-stamen,
ring out biology's religion
that all life-forms are one
so in the hump-backed fields
where roses graft from bone
the dead flower into life,
in unsuspecting form drawn on
towards their unimagined region.

VI

Beyond Monks' Gate

Seeing in the ruins of their abbeys
how their god made them unhappy
because men exacted the wrong tribute
the whipped dogs' devotion to the absolute
so faces turned to the wall, the statues wept,
closed ears to birdsong, eyes to the green
explosion of spring that had no text
drowned by the murmuration of prayer.

Standing on a stone is not a pilgrimage
nor on ceremony, the ritual implications
to civilise the tribe, to purify
with holy water. Yet water flows.
Love moves, as hands cross frontiers,
caress, clasp others, not one's own.

Yet the still centre's necessity, the beginning,
the place to depart from, the impetus
behind the energy that split the sky,
lightning that hurled down the spire
collapsed the tower into the overcrowded nave
was not an act of god. Did they accuse him
in their failure to build adequately, to rebuild
to fall again, the child's hand toppling the cards
stacked against one, in the unconsecrated continuum
science would occupy? Now with the geiger counter
we carbon date their faith and celebrate
the toppled mass, the absent host.

IV
ALMOST ALL
ELEGIES

Remembering John Tripp

> . . . *the hung dust*
> *of sorrow, how it lingers*
> *in rooms, on a road or beach,*
> *at the edges of celebration.*

A terrible loss—that cliché's spiked with irony
                    remembering you reading
'Ashes on the Cotswolds', how you helped a friend to scatter
                    the last of his sister-in-law
somewhere near Cleeve Hill, your poem's factual reportage
                    an antidote for grief, black humour
that ribs us all, but tickled your audience at the time.
                    Strange funerary instructions,
the urn carted round southern England, urgent as a car chase,
                    snatched from the crematorium
before it closed at noon on Saturday in Southampton.
                    Roast lamb for lunch at Salisbury,
the object on the back seat, its inescapable presence
                    impossible to defuse into reality.
But now time's overtaken you, its irrefutable shock
                    of wave, tide, clock
the rhetoric of the drowned when words aren't strong enough
                    for truth, simple and bare.
Memory's ash flies in the air, invisible everywhere,
                    finely lodges in clothes and hair,
becomes a voice reading, an audience listening. They sensed how
                    your uncompromising humour
realised the futility of it all;
                    even the wind of death on a hilltop
was claustrophobic. As one who heard you read
                    this poem, surrounded by polite
laughter reserved for the eccentricities of dying,
                    the truth we'd rather sweep
houseproud under the carpet like unwanted ashes,

>   who could anticipate
> I'd soon be watching the curtain glide
>   across your flamebound coffin
> in a last trick of theatre, ironic smile on bowing out?

Elegy for Ian Rodger

I

Your door closes
shutting out starlight
and homeward singing.

Witnessing terminal illness
your garden fought for breath
choked by the weeds' conspiracy.

Ten miles beyond, the Chilterns' line,
inviolate in haze, beamed messages
which a destroyed voice received,

could not transmit. And your refusal
to write in a nerve-shattered hand
an admission of dying

preferred a smile's defiance, eyes lit up
with deathless laughter, mouthing jokes
we tried too hard to understand.

Thus I reproach myself with the cowardice
of returning too late, of saying
and doing too little: of sympathy

that turns its back, hiding tears;
the knowledge that when a friend is dying
we all die too, our memories

burn in the air, decay into ground,
pray for absolution where none is found
for messages that never can be sent.

II

So, under the brooding windmill tower,
beneath its sails' quiescent shadows,
we scattered your ashes on common land.

On that brilliantly clear day
one should have observed the frontiers of the universe
from that common's microcosm.

Life should be more
than a handful of dust in the wind,
grey granules of ash in a white plastic pot

in which my fumbling hand touches the last of you,
grasps the elusive handful as a ringed bird released
down a small eddying breeze the direction of grief

in a puff of feathery grey, then falls to the ground,
its end invisible as a rainbow's base,
time's evanescence: ephemeral

moments held by life in its unconsidering sieve
and the words refractory, conventional, desperate not to give
way to a personal whimpering in the dark.

Grief's a blank wall: nothing to look
for but necessary whitewash defacing the memory's graffiti
in its urge to forget even courage and dignity.

III

Axes cut down our words:
cleavage of shared memories
arrested all growth
but the solitariness is worst
so great a gap in living
that the best of one's torn out.

Immortal in my mind
his cheerfulness transcended dying,
the tragedy reserved for other people.
He was a child of the sun
exuding lifeforce, outside contracting shadows
a visionary on a hilltop, the open land
confiding its secrets, and in his blood
the collective consciousness of history
informed by love, its generosity
and its weakness.

For me, a lesson to be learnt:
dependency's too much like ivy
caught up in the branches
of a dead tree.

Cricket in the Woods
(A Commentary in Green and White)

The white pavilions play at hide and seek in the green woods.
Their palings glint and give away the game that their shadows are
                                                        playing.
The sun's delicate glance through the branches of trees
intersects the boundary of blue sky
filtering through a leaf-green palimpsest
as the stippled balconies ripple with dainty applause.
Not quite off the middle of the bat,
memory retrieves the scene like a ball in long grass.
Tea-cups chatter on wobbly saucers, cucumber sandwiches are butter-
                                                        fingered,
tin numbers tremble on the tenterhooks of the breeze
fanning the dozers in deck-chairs, sleepers with handkerchief faces
as the scoreboard creaks on towards its late afternoon declaration.
A sunshaft's limelight pierces the trees' defensive field
to bounce off white sightscreens
in front of which immaculate flannels flash to and fro
with the movements of swallows, to dart in and pick up and throw.
A shouted appeal and the figures are frozen for a second's still frame.
A century ago, high seriousness rhymed with playing the game,
the eyes unflinching beneath striped caps,
the stiff upper lips under whiskers, and beards broad as Grace,
in the carefully posed profiles of teams in their sepia frame
and foxed mounting on each locker-room's white planking partitions.
In that cobwebby gloom laced by trees overhead
memory's odour is linseed for bats,
oil for roller and mower, chalk for the pads
and for the boundary-line, crease-marking machine.
Mown grass round the back wafts up dust of stale hay.
Out on the square the umpires starched in white coats
watch the upright take guard with a two-eyed stance.
A tiny red ball's the anomalous fruit of a game

that's otherwise played in two primary colours,
picked out by quickness of eye, and with a sharpness of ear
for the snick that's a catch at the wicket
though the hollow pock of a dead bat on the ball
won't wake the pavilioned sleepers at all
except for the rattle of stumps that cartwheel
to a shout of appeal as the bails fly into the air
with the last man out there, playing out time
in front of the sky's colour-change as the sun
ambles back into his cloud-pavilion,
raises his bat to applause, bolting down shutters and doors
into silence and night and white moonlight
so that no-one remembers the scores.

Soon there's a different rhythm:
a rustling in the trees, another underfoot,
the darkness crackling twigs, bead-eyes
of secretive creatures, owl-hoots, and wings
that flap across a prying moon.
The trees invade the pitch, their roots
will penetrate the square;
perhaps they're fielding, walking slowly in
from the boundary as the moon
runs in to bowl. No doubt
they'll try to catch some careless stars
in twig-fingered branches. Then, should clouds come in,
bad light stop play, shadows will multiply and link their arms
to embrace the white pavilions who'll escape,
eager as lovers, into the ever-darkening woods,
become absorbed into the territory of dreams
to go wherever wasted years have gone,
enlivening score-books' factual tedium,
set up new records. They'll bear witness to the runs
we never made, the wickets never taken, the missed chances,
the matches we should have won.

V
NATURAL
CAUSES

February Birds

In perching pairs
crotchets in branches
and on the horizontal bars
trapeze
the television aerials
ride the crosstrees
of messages
on telegraph poles
frozen in a static
two-fingered
contempt.
Droppings of song
smear parked cars
glaze double glazed windows
peck frozen-faced butts.
On staves of telephone wires
a sudden congregation
arrives for St. Valentine
with neither feast nor church
but on the line
for a mating call.

Bidden to the Feast

Still rosycheeked these wrinkled apple faces
shrunken in age of windscoured outdoor men
huddle together in the racks
leaning towards one another to exchange
old age's whispered confidences.

Perhaps they recall
the first darkness
in blossom's womb
broken open into sunlight
in sky's blue simplicity
in greenleafed frame
above the parched red
ploughed Hereford earth,
the swaying orchard
grown inaccessibly tempting
to schoolboys mitching,
the farmer with his stick
lurking behind the hedge,
before the final days
swung in the high trees
bounced by the wind
to a bruising fall.

Now in convict stripes
red pencil-thin on a green suit
wear prisoner's uniform indoors
for youth's green sharpness punished,
hardened off as long forgotten fruit
exiled from mother tree
into a mellowed age.
Each day survivors count

their comrades' disappearance, one by one
from the long rack
as if to execution:
no comfort in the poet's saying
Ripeness is all.

Treehouses

Rooktrees: listen how
their nest baskets
creak in the swing
of wickerwork branches;
here, winter's vacant premises
booked for spring letting's

prompt redecoration
wherever blue ceilings
blend into leafgreen,
where cot curtains rustle
in the fledgling wind's
lullaby; built high
towards the summer sun

too tall for serpent boys
dared up for eggs
or to haul roped planks
into the lowest treefork
clumsy as greenhorn sailors
whose treeship pitches
and lurches in the gale

and whose untrained fall's
inevitable in the wrong
element; unroped descent
from a birdless house,
planks slipped from the noose
catching ankle or neck,
on the slumped deck
dispossessed, mutinous.

Totentanz in May

Frühlingsgold
shakes her
curling-papered head,
the wind's
premature blow-drier
scattering news
of dispersed beauty,
the white petals
leaving the golden heart
on each stem:
first rose,
first dancer
to take the stage,
curtseys low
after her brief
pas seul.

Trainscape

Shaken out of trains,
reflected in windows,
the landscape moves,
shifts as clouds do,
as shadows race
across sun-shafted fields:
that early April rape's
a mere caress of yellow
streaking a sea of green;
closer, it's pointillism
waving dots
on a gentle brush of wind;
a scarecrow by a hedge,
that lightning-splintered tree's
protesting arms from fractured trunk's
a signpost pointing to
a lost direction
where all's green brilliance
of April-opened leaves, new paint
on an old pavilion.
This summer's team
has taken to the field;
the bowler starts his run-up,
but we've gone
into another frame;
a rabbit bounces out
beside the line,
leaps back into its burrow.
Our sudden tunnel's eye-blink view
shows how perspectives narrow
lurching and rattling through.

VI
MORE PLACES
THAN FACES

Rhondda Roundabout

Handholding houses
hopscotch down streets
to greyjerseyed chapels

Hoops bowl along
frostmetalled roads
whirring like winding-gear
though the pit's closed

The Rec's ashenfaced
as empty swings
snap fingers
at the creaking wind

Brassknobbled bedsteads
play harps in the river;
tin cans
rock and roll
on its stones

Bracchi's steamed up
for a coffee trip;
brass boilers gleam
with polish and spit
but no trains run,
Barry Island, Porthcawl,
both off the menu

Deserted platforms
vibrate with the silence
of cancelled meetings;

the Institute's
paper orators'
borrowed words
aren't returned

Neatly permed sheep
knit up their breakfast,
a short back and sides
on unlatched lawns

Pitpropped underground,
the treeless hillside
wrinkles into streams
on its slopes' sour turf
where whippets race after
rumours of rabbits

Roundshouldered hills
pack down for the night,
find a safe touch
with the spiralling moon

Only the pigeons
are racing certainties;
they fly off to England
and never come back.

Exodus From Blaenavon

A mined-out community. No miracles
could call it back to life. Abandoned seams
have settled their dust on the work ethic.
Big Pit's now a museum. Its winding-gear squeals

in the wheelhouse while you gently descend
in a canary-green cage. It's a mere three hundred feet
to shaft bottom, and then over slippery rails
to the five-foot face. Across the valley
scaffolding masks rebuilding at the ironworks.
Between them the compact trading estate
pretends there's a future, down a dead end.
In Blaenavon's heyday, happiness meant staying alive,
raising children under a passably dry roof,
keeping a fire in the grate, food in the larder,
and the front doorstep scrubbed spotless.
Cleanliness rubbed shoulders with Godliness
in a tin bath on the kitchen floor. The one hope,
faith in the World to Come: crossing Jordan,
taking the Minister's Word for it
in the full-throated chapel, even beside
slanting headstones in the shallow graveyard.
At a funeral, any faint rumble would make
the hand tremble holding the hymn-book.
After firedamp, hellfire flickered. But inside,
the singing stayed upright. Subsidence,
clawing upwards, resurrection's paradox,
splintered the road like a mirror in the rain.
Crazed too as old china the sepia photographs
recording the hardlined, bluescarred lives
screwed down inside pit darkness,
the rows of stalls like terraced houses.
After day-shift they'd climb to starlight
sprinkling the wintry smokehaze in a narrow bed
of sky like mourning crêpe. The coffin-lid
was being hammered down. Its nails were shining.

Endgame in Moffat Cemetery

Above a chequerpattern of flat slabs
obsessive funerary chessmen rise
from ornate graves with fretted carving,
crocketed rivals for height's prestige
for pawns who've reached their final square
on a board too crowded now for moves.

Death's stalemate long ago has locked
these players tight into its prison squares:
the famous one, Macadam,
genius of surfaces,
tarblack king on this board,
built and then took the same last road
as these two coachmen who in the blizzard dark
threw up their lives beneath the toppled Glasgow Mail,
unhorsed white knights whose shrouds were drifts,
whose second burial here won't thaw these stones
that mark the end of travelling, record no distances,
but paid for by the public
who left a similar honorarium for
the local physician carried off by cholera
though watched their cleric raise his tomb,
outlive two wives and seven children,
into whose overcrowded vault he slid
two days before his eighth and last child died;
Brontë survivor without biographer
he never made the bishop's move to gracious living.

The stark instructions of inscriptions
tell us the game was played but not its rules;
with white to play and mate in one
where is the stone-faced cheat who'll overturn the board?
On whose ninth square Thy Kingdom, Lord?

In Barbara Hepworth's Sculpture Garden, Trewin, St. Ives

Conversation pieces, still life that's never still.
Restless under shadows, sunshafts breaking through
the flickering leaves, these sculptures in the garden
confide in each other. In the night,
the garden gates, the back door of the house
being locked, they're changing places. Returned
at dawn to the familiar stance, see the brilliant
blue bowl of light reflecting over the water
from Godrevy; nearer, the white walls, slate roofs
of St. Ives shining in the morning. Brisk clouds
divide the shadows, tree-branches in the wind
opening and closing curtains. Now
the upright forms are silent, drawing in their breath
as in a theatre, about to speak their opening lines.
Some dressed in marbled veins of blood
affirm Greek tragedy. Trees, flowers,
speaking with bird-song voice the chorus, will set off
each movement that's within a stillness.
Listen. The wind drops suddenly. The play begins.

At Higher Bockhampton

Arrived for your birth a hundred and fifty
years late, Wise Man only from hindsight,
bringing no gift but admiration:
the house framed as in the mind's picture,
trees cradling it, rocking your sleep
with pine-winds' sighing, and at the sun's
march towards afternoon, a lullaby of bees.
A place of frontiers: the first is yours,
the middle room upstairs where the midwife
kindled life's spark from apparent stillbirth,
saved you for history. Such chances determine
the plots of your novels, where living
isn't the luck we'd hope it might be.
Desperate Remedies, Victorian Gothic
architecture embellished by the melodramatic,
this earliest begun on the next window-sill
to this, where I rested my hand
in the grip of your writing fingers
whose story uncurls as a fern's frost-flowers
on the window-pane, clawing at shivering glass,
imprisoned by cold, inside and out,
deaths coming too soon, out of unreason,
the snapped bone, tubercular blood coughed up,
familiar recitals of hereditary disease.
Living on nature's frontier here
a second tense dividing line,
below, Froom Valley; above, Egdon Heath:
the opposites in you were natural ironies,
landscapes in character. Learning to write it,
as harsh a struggle as living here in winter,
despite sufficiency above your relatives'
poverty in dirt and drink in Puddletown.

Later, you'd shut your doors to them, married to
an archdeacon's niece, but part of you
went straying home to earthy stories
flickering about the fireside, ancestral voices
amid smoke rising, crackling with laughter.
Behind the house, the Heath's murmurings
deterred unwelcome visitors behind the blind
rear cottage wall that turned a windowless back
on nature, indifferent, hostile even,
on territory still unclaimed until
your middle age, where ghosts refused an exorcism.
Walking with Grandmother: *Domicilium*;
much later, *Neutral Tones*: Tryphena at the pond,
a landscape shrunken inside itself
to wintry grey; love frosted out,
a wreath of blackened flowers.
Perhaps in you this always would be so.
What was shut away inside you
escaped into fiction, a life rewritten:
'T.H. by F.E.H.' gave nothing away.
Death brought ironies, further divisions,
two funerals, Westminster Abbey for your ashes,
your unconsumed heart beside Emma at Stinsford
where you'd lately said you'd wanted to be,
absolving the latter neglect, your regret
for an early love's withering, 'Woman much missed':
later, a flushed stout woman on a bicycle
unsteady in High Street, Dorchester,
feet off the pedals, free-wheeling downhill
with the skirt-lifting wind revealing her bloomers;
short-tempered with tradesmen, you at writing
behind locked doors in a silent room

in chilly, bathroom-less Max Gate,
the house you designed for yourself:
house, not a home, as your birthplace reminds us.
Love's second chance, too late, just as elusive:
Florence soured into loneliness,
still protecting you from all callers,
crept in beside you, less than a decade
after your death. So your heart's between two,
yet whom did you wish for lying with you?
So many secrets; all the letters
had been safely burnt, following your instructions,
then *The Life* published. Now on the wintry side,
the agnostic north of Stinsford's churchyard,
the Hardy family tombs are neatly aligned.
From the exterior, squat-towered, with its flat
roofed north aisle, the church must have offended
your architect's precise proportions.
Surely after the poetry of your birthplace,
a somewhat prosaic concluding chapter,
its unprepossessing appearance
a portrait of yourself in middle age
as seen by Strang or Blanche, with drooping moustache
and eyes cast down, 'Little Thomas Hardy'.
But like your own, the church's interior's
an unexpected vision. Here where you sat
beneath the plaque commemorating Angel Grey
whose name you took for Tess's Angel, Clare
in his madness of morality, you struggled with
your unbelief that alienated Emma.
From Stinsford it's further to Max Gate
than to Higher Bockhampton, but from both
a fair step, easier on your bicycle.
Suddenly awheel, plus-foured, you'd become

a modern writer. It's your span
of nearly ninety years that stops us short:
who nearly died at birth, the weakest one
who lasted longest, as your writing will.

VII
TICKLING
THE
IRONIES

Old Yuppaeans' Boating Song

Success flows through
the river's laughing images,
negotiating weirs
like business deals
without parting company
where the painted banks
are aflame with guilt's
inflated proscriptions:
hire what you need
but paddle your own canoe.

Mirrors will show
the necessary confidence
driving past in the wrong lane,
anticipating rain
from a clear blue sky:
since the blind will pick you out
at love's identity parade,
pretend not to care a damn
who might as well be hanged
for a sheep as a lamb.

Gaudeamus, Regurgitur

Bullies with drawn teeth, edentulous dribblers
fumbling after drinks and young girls or one
once handsomely athletic with Greek God profile
now leaning on a stick, bald, and wrinkled
like a shrunken apple: roll call of the old gang,
Auden's ruined boys answering their names,
others putting on the defiant face
of not remembering too much.
We ask each other what we did with life.
It passed us by so quickly, on the other side.
Questioning obliquely those hearsay deaths
that no-one likes to mention as we're wondering
what's left to us, we notice some are far from well,
kept in too long in life's interminable
detention class. Better recall the trivia,
always getting the joke a bit wrong, but
they all know it off by heart anyway,
lest the truth rears off a good length,
poleaxes us between the eyes.
Laughter is safely esoteric and excludes
the outsider from the team. Each brings the endless
boredom of his recent news, stretched out
like telephone wires beside a railway line
though all the trains have ceased to run.
Because we treat each meeting as our last,
the child's compelled to go on listening, be a man.
We still distrust our adolescent selves and memories
of others' selves. Initiation ceremonies of the tribe
ensure next generation's pain, keep us alive.

Marketing Eternity

Cathedrals set out their wares
along their West Shop Fronts:
carved saints for sale in their niches
luring the gullible, credulous buyers;
such mediaeval advertising's permanent
for they can't carry away the statues
impersonating what's for sale
within the welcome of the Galilee
where silvery pilgrim fish swarm into the net.
But it's at the sharp East End
that the serious business is done
in intimate chantries purchasing absolution,
masses said for the soul, prayers repeated,
candles lit and relics kissed:
the money-changers haven't been missed.

Heartbreak House Revisited

(G.B. Shaw, Preface to *Heartbreak House*)

I: Shooting Parties

The Red Flag's flying over butts.
His Majesty has fired the course:
some capital shots; gun-dogs bring in
maimed partridge like the sad-eyed peasantry
while lolling, casual soldiery
smoking off guard, lean on the turf embrasures,
each with his *Manual of Rifle Drill*
kept buttoned in a stiff-necked uniform
scarlet as a revolutionary text,
the only colour not to show up blood.
His Majesty is praised for a straight aim,
his strong right arm extending a firm grip,
his eyes narrowing into gun-metal.
His host's perfunctory nod with military despatch
consigns each neatly labelled carcase to
scrubbed larder, whitewashed cellar: not on order,
a brace of corpses in the mortuary;
inverted dogma turning wine to blood,
a miracle becomes an accident.
Whenever firing squads are practising
heads should be kept below the parapet
and eyes averted, modestly, of course.
The beaters are expendable
as Other Ranks whistled over the top
at the Royal Pleasure. Perhaps it isn't
musketry crackling in the distance
but the Lodge put to the torch, park gates unhinged.

66

At the long drive's end, complacency's
unjustifiable despite the dignity
of statuary and fountains fronting the Great House
from whose roof's leads the Royal Standard's broken
but out of sight of history's perspective.
Outside the gun-room children play with matches.
Conspiracy may draw short straws
in city tenements; but for Gentlemen
words are preferred to do the killing,
the paper knives assassinating character.
Duelling at dawn's become unpopular.
The Palace Guards' uneasy drill will countermarch
beneath slow-moving skies, revengeful rain piled up.
The August shooting-parties, fearing wires are cut,
exchange frenetic telegrams in code:
Cease firing. Stop. Troop movements blocking road.

II: Nocturne at the Manor

Sometimes
        when opening
            a door
you can hear
        darkness marching
                up and down outside
its footsteps
        scuffing up gravel
while moonlit shadows
        form fours
            in trees
whose branches trail
        streamers of starlight

67

Whatever's outside
        unseen for a moment
dispositions unready
        house-guests
            from upper windows
discharging both barrels
        their aim unsteady

It's the supreme
        powerful
irrational out there
        whispering
            igniting fear
like cottage burnings
        on shuttered estates
            on the far side
of an innocent country

        And frightening
            as God talking

III: Bal Masqué

Foxtrot and Charleston
slink by on the terrace;
a paper moon
croons in the trees.

Downslope, the river
draws a shawl of mist
over its shoulders,
inhaling its territory.

On rebarbative plains
beyond, drums dance to
ululations, hoofbeats,
the Alamo's burning arrows.

Belated messenger up here,
the starlight telegraphs
the glass brilliance
of shattering chandeliers,

lights going out
upstairs, downstairs;
in smouldering darkness,
an aroma of cigar-ash.

The bobbling moon's
face-down in the fountain
where naked revellers
have turned to stone.

The Chairs

Once you begin, things come easily enough, like life and death . . . you just have to
make up your mind. It's as we speak that we find our ideas, our words, ourselves, too,
in our own words, and the city, the garden, perhaps everything comes back and we're
not orphans any more.

(Eugène Ionesco, The Chairs)

I: Garden Party

The chairs stand around in the garden.
They hold their glasses tucked into their bodies.
They are conversation pieces, casually grouped.
Their white teeth smile in polished slats.
Arms rest on hips. In a firm stance
they plant their legs astride on a claimed plot,
not to be easily shifted.
                        Notwithstanding,
left out in the rain at night an unsuspected wind
will find them lying on their backs in the morning
as if scattered after a party, but with no homes
to go to, in their inchoate revelling
a soft touch, a pushover after it.
                           They have become
the people who sat on them.

II. The Party's Over

Hurled into the back of the van with shutters up
they lie in tangled interlocking matchstick limbs
with the innocence of corpses out of Auschwitz:
eyes fixedly staring, glazed,
flyblown in death's accusing stare,
skullheads turned upwards,
twisted on rackstretched necks
towards the interrogating light.

A splintered word
carelessly thrown in like a match
would ignite the bonfire, explode the petrol tank,
melt plastic down to bone and rubbery stench.
After that, silence, soon to be ash
in the crematoria.
                    Handle them carefully, then,
as if they were people.

III: At the Saluting Base

The chairs turn back to back,
move to the right in threes, attack,
left wheel, form fours, retreat,
then halt!, right dress, make signs,
straightening the snaking lines.
They stand at ease, then squat,
become an audience, en bloc.
A smaller group's detached itself, complete,
appears on-stage (one-time saluting base),
confronts the audience face to face,
then moves like actors noiselessly
on well-oiled castors (not to try
the dodgem drama, bump and yell!)
One wonders who is entertaining whom.
The parade ground's now an audience room.
A throne stands in the middle for
the Emperor or the Orator.
Which one will enter first one cannot tell.

Soldiers, actors, clowns and courtiers
behave according to set formulas,
are like deaf mutes, immaculate,
mechanical, and never late.
But when the drama grows absurd,
the Orator speaking not a word,
the chairs turn round: *Revenge!* they cry,
eschew this stark formality;
we have been sat upon too long
by language morally as wrong.

Origami

I

Perhaps you'll hear
a voice dictating
a complete poem
word-perfect:

or a rhythm beating out
spaces that words fall into
like soldiers forming up
on a parade-ground,
the letters' military lines
strutting across the page,
typewriter's heels clicking:

or on scraps of paper,
backs of envelopes
at bedside, scribbling
in the darkness, in the morning

awakening to a scrawl,
the memory illegible:

also from tops of buses
how people and scenery
refract, dissolve
in polished surfaces
within the frames
of mirror-images
you've noted down on backs
of tickets, to be blown away
through an open window
as the inspector
climbs the stairs:

so you're turned off
into streets awash with paper
after Saturday's carnival
wore paper hats of poetry
with a throwaway ending.

II

The soldiers fall out,
disperse to barrack room
or wet canteen;
pieces of paper blow
across a deserted
parade-ground;
a surge of brass
as the band-practice room
opens its door:

each bus has forgotten
its day's passengers, sleeps
in its allotted row
inside the depot's darkness
under frosted-glass roofing
that admits a furred moon
to share the night's terminus:

outside, street cleaners
have long swept up
and put the carnival to bed:

but a poem drains away
down the black hole
of a misplaced image
into abstraction:

yet its pattern
although it's been cut
out of alignment
and in the wrong dimension
is persistent
as insomnia.

III

Ordered to begin again
shaping a new poem from the matrix,
taking care to cut along the lines,
you'll sift pared off, spare images
littering the workshop floor
the first drafts drifting through the door;
inside the workroom, scissors gouge
malicious splinters from the drawing-board,

wastepaper baskets choke
on a feast of rejected words:

so take the poem home
to play it through
from holes that punctuate
the pianola roll
but don't expect music
to sing without hands:

if your house should be tone-deaf
after carnivals
or military bands
take out the poem
for a walk on a lead
to let it bark
at disconcerted strangers;
but then go on
where no one's listening
except yourself.

IV

Writing is waiting;
but paper's knife-edged
gashing the fingers
with a leap of blood
for words on the page,
a white and red jostling
of unlucky flowers:

too soon now the manuscript
will lie in the fireplace
for the innocent housemaid
to strike a match:

outside, the garden
coughs bonfire smoke,
grey flecks from the embassy
question-mark skywards:

in drawing room,
library, garden,
conversations fragment
like tea-cups shattering
into silence at sounds
of subliminal gunfire
for it's autumn and no one's
been reading the leaves:

as to the future
erase, revise,
words for the wise
swallowing memory;
how long is it
meant to last, anyway?

Fathers' Race

Your feet trip over each other at the starter's pistol.
They are tied together in a sack. Convulsively nervous
as you fall full length, the china egg
flies from its spoon, bounces and smashes
into the floral dresses and pin-stripe suits
who, lining the track, duck straw-hatted heads
in polite, egg-stained laughter. You stagger to your feet,
climb out of the sack, and your trousers fall down.
Far off, complaisant Fathers go hobblety-hop,
kangarooing it off on an outback trail
to the distant finishing line which may be Australia.
But the crowd's watching *you*.

After a twinkling of tea-cups, a stodging of buns,
the headmaster's wife is presenting the prizes
under the awning in front of the yawning marquee.
Spruced up for the ceremony when they call out the winners—
Fathers' Race, next! (Human Race, later)—you stride to the daïs
in glossy top hat and—just back from the cleaners'—
your one birthday suit, impeccably pressed.
You formally bow to the headmaster's wife
presenting a cabbage, fist-tight, football-round,
predestined school dinners you never forgot.
Her eyes look straight through you, just like your wife's
(last seen with your son and a *muscular* man).
Whoever should notice, nobody cares,
when no-one, not even yourself,
knows whether they're dreaming or not.

Farewell Performance

Not even a walking-on part before
your no-score years and then

you're one of the old who read
in a creaking voice

against a thin-lipped matinée's
tintinnabulating tea-cups—

my old bone-shaking China,
the wife says, idolised too late

in a silence when the unpronounceable
dribbles like saliva,

meaning's necklace-string shattering,
pearly spittle over starched-front stalls,

until, at the end of the act,
you try your last trick,

memory shuffling
the visiting cards of the dead.

NOTES ON A FEW POEMS

Childhood's Country

Queen Alexandra Hospital, Cosham, near Portsmouth, is the hospital referred to in 'A Sheltered Upbringing'. It took in its first patients, war wounded soldiers, in 1908, but is now a general hospital.

Constructed at the beginning of this century, the Horndean Tramway eventually ran from South Parade Pier, Southsea, to Horndean, but was dismantled in 1935. In appearance it resembled the Seaton to Colyton Tramway in South Devon still in use today.

The Portsdown Hill Forts were constructed between 1860 and 1868 to protect Portsmouth Harbour and its naval base from landward attack. French military power had increased considerably under Napoleon III so that an invasion scare resulted.

Classical Studies

'An Appointment with Mithras' is autobiographical. 'Your terrible death' refers to Ian Rodger, radio dramatist, novelist and critic who died from motor neurone disease in 1984 (*vide* 'Elegy to Ian Rodger'.)

According to the archaeologist T.C. Lethbridge, the Cerne Abbas Giant, pre-Roman in origin, originally had a female partner, now two feet under grass. The Giant's 30-foot phallus pointed to sunrise on the crest of the hill on May Day, near which spot Maypole dancing would take place on that day until the Puritans prohibited it in 1635.

Peals and Changes

For the legend of Seithennin (or Seithenyn) I refer readers to the entry under Cantre'r Gwaelod in *The Oxford Companion to the Literature of Wales, ed.* Meic Stephens, p. 71. The inundation of Gwyddno Garanhir's kingdom is, for me, a paradigm for Viking raids in Cardigan Bay. The sarnau, originally thought to be man-made sea defences, are flat outcrops of rock running westwards and parallel to each other out into Cardigan Bay and are uncovered at low tide. Sarn Gynfelin is the southernmost and nearest to Aberystwyth.

Almost All Elegies

In 'Remembering John Tripp', the epigraph is taken from his 'Death of a Father', *Passing Through*, (Poetry Wales Press, 1984), in which collection 'Ashes on the Cotswolds' can be found on p. 19.

Tickling the Ironies

Eugène Ionesco, a Rumanian expatriate who lived in Paris, wrote in French. Perhaps his play *The Chairs* is linguistic transubstantiation, 'chair' being French for 'flesh'. As in Ionesco's play, my chairs become flesh, i.e. people. Section III of this sequence makes particular reference to the action of the play.

79